A Bear for Bimi

A Bear for Bimi

By Jane Breskin Zalben

Illustrated by Yevgenia Nayberg

KAR-BEN
PUBLISHING

KAR-BEN PUBLISHING®
An imprint of Lerner Publishing Group, Inc.
241 First Avenue North
Minneapolis, MN 55401 USA

Website address: www.karben.com

Main body text set in Adobe Caslon Pro.
Typeface provided by Adobe Systems.

Library of Congress Cataloging-in-Publication Data

Names: Zalben, Jane Breskin, author. | Nayberg, Yevgenia, illustrator.
Title: A bear for Bimi / by Jane Breskin Zalben ; illustrated by Yevgenia Nayberg.
Description: Minneapolis, MN : Kar-Ben Publishing, an imprint of Lerner Publishing Group,
    Inc., [2021] | Includes notes on helping refugees and immigrants and on making stuffed
    bears. | Audience: Ages 4–8. | Audience: Grades K–1. | Summary: "When Bimi's family
    immigrates to America and moves into Evie's neighborhood, not everybody is welcoming.
    But with the help of kind neighbors and a teddy bear, a friendship is born"– Provided by
    publisher.
Identifiers: LCCN 2020040467 (print) | LCCN 2020040468 (ebook) | ISBN 9781728415710
    (hardcover) | ISBN 9781728415727 (paperback) | ISBN 9781728428918 (ebook)
Subjects: CYAC: Neighborliness–Fiction. | Emigration and immigration–Fiction. | Jews–United
    States–Fiction. | Muslims–United States–Fiction.
Classification: LCC PZ7.Z254 Bb 2021 (print) | LCC PZ7.Z254 (ebook) | DDC [E]–dc23

LC record available at https://lccn.loc.gov/2020040467
LC ebook record available at https://lccn.loc.gov/2020040468

Manufactured in the United States of America
1-48686-49104-1/11/2021

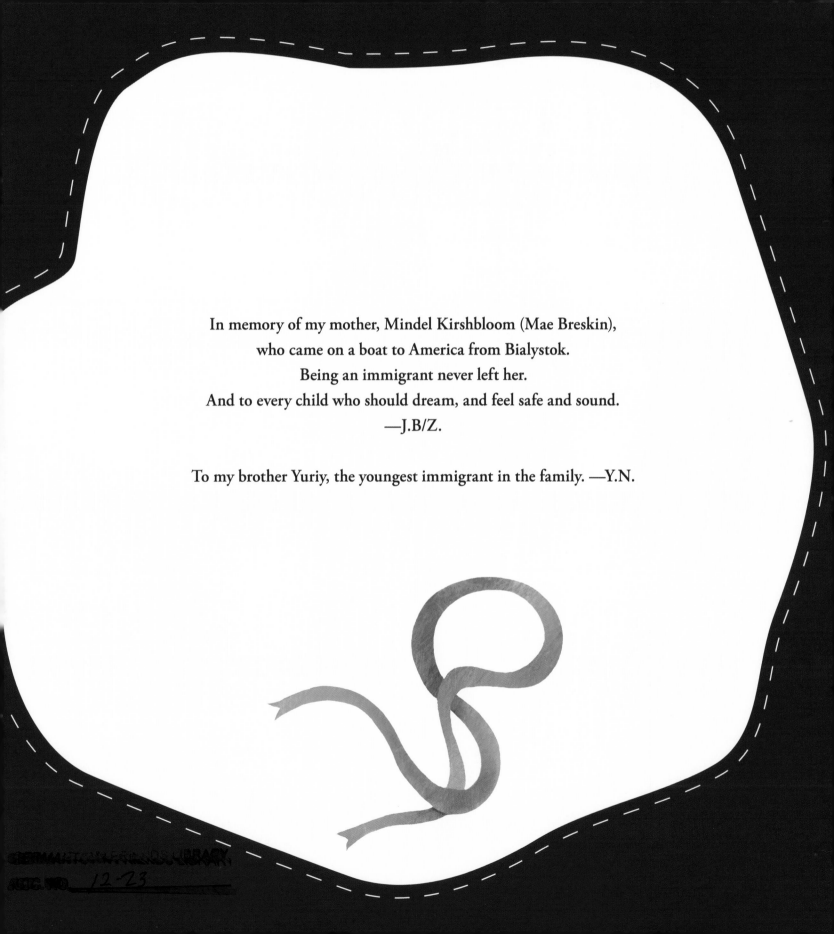

In memory of my mother, Mindel Kirshbloom (Mae Breskin),
who came on a boat to America from Bialystok.
Being an immigrant never left her.
And to every child who should dream, and feel safe and sound.
—J.B/Z.

To my brother Yuriy, the youngest immigrant in the family. —Y.N.

One golden, brisk autumn day, Mama told Evie,
"A family from far away is moving in next door."
"People from another country," added Papa.

"Like Grandpa and Grandma?" asked Evie.
"Yes, Evie. Like them."
A week later, a van pulled up to the curb.

Evie ran outside into the chilled air. "Hello!"
On the front lawn, inside a large cardboard box,
a boy sat, singing words Evie didn't understand.

"What's your name?" asked Evie. "Mine's Evie."
She pointed to herself.
"Bimi," said the boy, smiling shyly.

Bimi's father held two big cartons in his arms.
Papa volunteered to take the heavier one upstairs.
"Shukraan. Thank you. I am Ibrahim Said," said Bimi's father.
"And I'm Abe Gold." Evie's father gave a friendly nod.

Evie saw Mrs. Monroe from across the street peeking through her curtains, watching, with a strange look on her face. Bimi saw it too.

At dinner, Bimi told his parents. They sighed.

"Some people are scared of others who seem different," said Bimi's father.

"Until they get to know them," added Bimi's mother.

At dinner, Evie told her parents. They sighed.

"Mrs. Monroe wasn't born in America," said Evie's father.

"She should remember what it feels like," added Evie's mother.

That night, Evie saw a light glowing in Bimi's bedroom.
He was gazing at the moonlit sky out his window.

Evie waved to Bimi. Bimi waved back.
That gave Evie an idea.

In the morning, Evie asked, "Can we take some things to Bimi's family?"
"Oh, Evie." Mama gave her a kiss, and they gathered
coats and curtains and brought them next door.

Herbie, who lived downstairs from the Saids, offered a lamp,
while his roommate, Harry, carried in a table, then some chairs.
"Extra ones for guests someday!" He grinned widely.

Luca and Letty Lioni on the top floor
gave the Saids a quilt with bright stars and bold stripes.

The twins, Leo and Lucy, shared crayons, drawing paper, and books.

Their little cousins, who lived a block away, had an extra soccer ball.

Over the next few days, one neighbor told another about the new family.

The Schwartzes brought over dishes, cups, and silverware.
Their five daughters baked cherry strudel and a honey cake.

Fatima, from around the corner, treated the Saids like old friends, delivering a "Welcome" doormat from Pickles' Thrift Shop.

On the weekend, everyone squeezed around the Saids' table.
"See, you did need the extra chairs for guests!" said Harry.

The children went outside to play, jumping in a pile of crisp leaves, until they noticed Mrs. Monroe coming up the sidewalk. "Uh-oh!" whispered the twins.
Suddenly Mrs. Monroe's grocery shopping bag ripped open.

Fruit scattered and rolled toward Bimi's feet.
"Oh no!" gasped Evie.
Bimi stood frozen.

Then Bimi scooped up two shiny apples, a thick-skinned
orange, and some plump green grapes.
He extended his arms filled with fruit.
Mrs. Monroe hesitated.

Just then Bimi's mother opened her door. "Hello. As salam aleykum."
And she offered Mrs. Monroe a glass of mint tea and a slice of honey cake.
Mrs. Monroe said with an awkward smile, "Thank you."
"And thank *you* for bringing some fruit salad!" teased Mrs. Said.

With new neighbors around the Saids' table, Mrs. Said's voice trembled.
"We miss our family and old friends. We left in such a rush."
"But it's nice to have new ones," Mr. Said chimed in.
And he placed his hand over his heart.

That gave Evie another idea.

She ran home and got her favorite stuffed bear—
the brown one with crackled glass eyes.
When she returned, Evie handed it to Bimi.
"For me?" asked Bimi.

Smoothing her fingers over the bear's face, Evie nodded.
Bimi cradled the bear in his arms, its fur tickling his nose.
"It reminds me of the one I lost when we had to leave."

Bimi dipped his hand in his pocket and took out three round pebbles
the color of blue-and-green marbles,
the color of the sea he had crossed to get to his new home.
"From my grandmother's garden," he said, giving one to Evie.
"For me?" asked Evie.

Smoothing his fingers over the pebbles, Bimi nodded.
He kept one pebble and tucked the last one in the bear's pocket.
Evie took off her silk hair ribbon and tied it
around the bear's worn, much-loved neck.

"What's the bear's name?" asked Bimi.

"Evie," said Evie. "But it's your bear now.
What are you going to call it?"

Bimi said with a shy smile, "Still Evie."
Now Bimi knew he was home.
And so did Evie.

"Friendship marks a life even more deeply than love. . . .
Friendship is never anything but sharing. . . .
For me, every hour is grace. No human race is superior;
no religious faith is inferior."

—*Elie Wiesel*

"Love will find its way through all languages on its own."

—*Rumi*

"We can help make the world safe for diversity.
We all inhabit this small planet.
We all breathe the same air.
We all cherish our children's future.
And we are all mortal."

—*President John F. Kennedy,
in an address to the United Nations*

What You Can Do

Millions of people around the world have been forced to leave their homes because of the dangers of conflict or persecution. These refugees, especially children, feel a huge sense of loss. Many can never return to their homes. They must leave behind friends and relatives, their schools and neighborhoods, and nearly everything they own.

In the United States and around the world, many organizations exist to help *refugees*, who have fled danger, and *immigrants*, who have moved to a new country in search of better lives. If you want to help, you can look for groups like this in your community. You can also find websites for groups that work all over the country and even all over the world.

How to Make a Stuffed Bear

Many refugee and immigrant children face hardship and loneliness.

Having a stuffed animal as a friend, as Bimi and Evie do, can help children who have newly come to America to settle into their new homes.

With some help from an adult, you can make a stuffed bear for someone who needs one. (Or you can trace a picture of the bear for a friend.)

Materials

Pencil

Scissors

Piece of fabric twice the size of the template on the facing page

Needle and thread (or sewing machine)

Fiberfill stuffing

Permanent marker, buttons, or colored felt and glue

Ribbon to tie around bear's neck (optional)

Instructions

1. You will need an adult to help you with this project.
2. Take a piece of fabric twice the size of the teddy bear template on the facing page.
3. Fold the fabric in half, and trace the teddy bear template.
4. Cut out both pieces of the teddy bear.
5. Sew around the edges, leaving one side open for stuffing.
6. Turn the bear inside out.
7. Stuff with fiberfill.
8. Turn the right side out.
9. Carefully sew the opening shut.
10. Add the eyes, nose, and mouth with a permanent marker, by sewing on buttons for eyes, or by gluing colored felt for the eyes, nose, and mouth.
11. Tie a ribbon around the neck.

About the Author

Jane Breskin Zalben, an author, artist, and abstract painter, was born in New York City, went to the High School of Music & Art in Harlem, graduated from Queens College, and went on to study printmaking at the Pratt Graphics Center in Manhattan. She has created over fifty award-winning books for children. Her work has been exhibited in libraries, galleries, and museums. Her studio is on Long Island, New York.

About the Illustrator

Yevgenia Nayberg is an award-winning illustrator, painter, and stage designer. A native of Kiev, Ukraine, she graduated from the National School of Arts. She lives in New York City.